An Egg-stra Special Easter

By Meredith Rusu

SCHOLASTIC INC.

ISBN 978-1-338-30756-6

10 9 8 7 6 5 4 3 2 1   19 20 21 22 23

Printed in the U.S.A.   40
First printing 2019
Book design by Becky James

"Gather around!" Carrots the bunny announced. "It's time for my Easterific Egg Hunt!"

"Sp-egg-tacular!" cheered her Beanie Boo friends.

2

"An egg hunt?" asked a little lamb named Blossom. "How does it work?"

Posy the chick, Clover the lamb, Bugsy the ladybug, and Gabby the goat had all done the egg hunt before, but this was Blossom's very first Easter.

"I've hidden lots of colorful eggs around the farm," Carrots explained. "Inside each is an Easter surprise. Your job is to find the eggs! But you'll have to be quick, because when I blow my carrot whistle, the hunt is over."

4

"I can be quick!" promised Blossom. "I'll find an egg lickety-split!"
"Then it's time to get hopping!" said Carrots.
The Beanie Boos hurried over to the starting line.
"On your marks . . ." said Carrots. "Get set . . . not just Beanie Boo yet . . . GO!"

Off dashed the Beanie Boos! Some darted left. Some zipped right. But Blossom zoomed straight ahead. She knew the perfect place to look for an egg: the vegetable patch!

Blossom searched through rows of red tomatoes, clusters of orange carrots, and groups of yellow peppers. Then, sure enough . . .

"A purple egg!" Blossom cried. "I found one!"

Blossom reached for the shiny purple egg and pulled it from between the leaves.

Snap! To her surprise, she was holding . . .

An eggplant!

"Oh!" said Blossom, disappointed.

"Don't give up!" called a voice overhead. It was Bugsy the ladybug. "Try the pond. You'll have better luck there!"

"The pond!" Blossom wiggled her nose. She and Carrots had been playing there yesterday. Maybe Carrots hid an egg there, too! "Thanks, Bugsy!"

Blossom scampered off to the pond. She nudged her way through the cattails by the water. She pushed aside one rock and then another.

"There!" she finally shouted. "A sparkly egg! I knew it!"

She was pulling out the egg when . . .

"Hey! Do you mind?" Scooter the snail poked his head out from the egg, which wasn't an egg at all, but his shell!

"Oh, I'm sorry!" Blossom apologized. "I thought you were an Easter egg."

"That's okay," Scooter said with a yawn. "It happens every year. I'm too slow for egg hunts. But I guess I shouldn't nap during the hunt, either."

Just then, Gabby the goat came up over the hill. Her basket was piled high with colorful eggs.

Not far away, Clover was calling out, "I picked up a pink egg by the meadow! And look! Here's a blue one from the bushes!"

Blossom's eyes grew big with worry.

"What's wrong, Blossom?" Gabby asked.

Blossom sighed. "I haven't found any eggs yet. And everyone else is finding tons. Soon, there won't be any left."

"Don't worry," said Gabby. "It's your first egg hunt, after all. I'm sure you'll find one! Have you tried colorful places? Like the veggie patch? Or the flower garden?"

14

"The flower garden!" Blossom exclaimed. "I didn't think of that. I bet Carrots hid a bunch of eggs in the colorful flowers. Thanks, Gabby!"

With a burst of speed, Blossom dashed off.

Sure enough, as soon as Blossom reached the garden she spotted exactly what she was hoping for. A bright yellow egg was nestled between the daffodils.

"Woo-hoo! I finally found an egg!" Blossom cheered.

But just as she was reaching for it . . .

16

Posy the chick hopped out from the flowers and scooped up the egg first!

"Hey—that was my egg!" Blossom said.

"It was?" Posy asked. Her little beak quivered. "But this is the only egg I've found."

"Oh," said Blossom. She didn't want her friend to feel bad. "It's okay. You can keep it. You did reach it first."

Feeling sad, Blossom trudged to the barn and plopped down on a pile of hay. The Easterific Egg Hunt was almost over, and she hadn't found a single egg.

I guess I'll have to wait until next year, she thought.

Just then, Blossom heard a noise behind her.

It was Daisy the cow! "Moooooove," Daisy said. "You're sitting on—"

Blossom felt the hay beneath her. Could it be?
"It's an egg!" she said, hopping up. The egg was smooth and round and had a brown shell with white speckles.

"I finally found an egg!" Blossom cried. "I did it!"
"But—" Daisy started.
Wheeeeeee! Carrots's whistle blew.
Blossom put the egg in her basket. "Gotta go, Daisy! Thanks for helping me find my egg!"

19

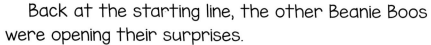

Back at the starting line, the other Beanie Boos were opening their surprises.

Clover's pink egg was filled with chocolate candies.

And Posy's yellow egg was overflowing with jellybeans.

"I wonder what's inside mine!" Blossom held up her brown egg with white speckles.

The Beanie Boos stared at Blossom's egg in surprise.

"Uh, Blossom," said Carrots. "I didn't hide *that* egg."

"You didn't?" asked Blossom. "But then how did it get in the barn?"

Suddenly, Blossom's egg began to rumble. It began to shake.

Crrrrraaaaaack!

Out popped a brand-new baby chick!

"Cheep-cheep!" said the chick. "I'm Goldie!"

"Aw, how sweet!" cooed Clover.

"Beanie-Boorrific!" cheered Bugsy.

"Blossom, your egg wasn't an Easter egg," said Carrots. "It was a *real* egg! You found the best Easter surprise of all!"

"I did?" Blossom asked, confused. Then she broke into a wide grin. "Yeah, I guess I did!"

Blossom nuzzled the little chick. "I found an egg-stra special Easter surprise—a new friend!"